SCARLET'S TALE

Written by **Audrey Vernick**

Illustrated by **Jarvis**

WILLIAMSBURG REGIONAL LIBRARY
7770 CROAKER ROAD
WILLIAMSBURG, VA 23188

APR – – 2021

DISNEP · HYPERION

LOS ANGELES   NEW YORK

When Scarlet was born, her parents did the usual counting.

Two eyes.

One nose.

Ten fingers.

Ten toes.

Also: one long, fluffy, fuzzy, furry tail.

That was a surprise.

Like most little babies, Scarlet couldn't talk.
But unlike the others, she made herself understood.

Her parents knew that Scarlet loved dogs.

And the color red.

That it was exciting
to be sudsed up
into a soapy snowman.

And there was
nothing better than
swinging in the yard,
watching the sun shine
through the leaves.

Sure, there were challenges.

Her clothes had to be
custom-made, to allow
a fluffy, fuzzy, furry tail
to poke through.

And once Scarlet learned to walk,
low shelves needed to be cleared off.
Her parents became very skilled at
tail holes and rearranging.

Her parents were happy
to do it. So Scarlet was
happy, too.

my family

Life at home was pretty great.

But on Scarlet's
first day of preschool,
things got less great.

Kids stared.

Some grown-ups
did, too.

Scarlet didn't want
her parents to leave.

But they did.
It was a hard day.

At circle time, the other kids kept pointing at Scarlet's tail.

Scarlet decided to sit on it.
That worked.

Until snack time.

Scarlet's tail went wild.
It slapped the teacher's hands,
sending all the cookies flying.

And that wasn't all.
Scarlet's tail knocked things off
tables.
And shelves.
And benches.
And chairs.

At pick-up time, the teacher
asked each child to name
the best part of her day.

"Right now," Scarlet said
as she ran out the door.

The next day,
Scarlet played by herself.

When she climbed on a swing,
she could feel Callie and Josh watching.

She was lonely, but as she started to move back and forth
and watched the sun shimmering through the leaves,
her tail started wagging. Slowly.

Callie and Josh
started to smile.

Scarlet pumped the
swing higher and her
tail wagged faster.

Callie's and Josh's
smiles grew bigger.

And when Callie and Josh climbed on the swings
next to Scarlet, her wagging tail pushed her higher still.

From that day on,
Scarlet and Callie and Josh
were together at all the times:

circle,

free,

snack,

story.

Each morning, when Scarlet spotted her
friends walking into the classroom,
her tail would wag back and forth
super fast until it was nearly
moving in circles.

Sometimes Callie and Josh
would wag their own behinds.
And so would all the
kids watching them.

Before long, most kids at Scarlet's school
wagged their behinds when
they were happy.

It was a very waggy school.

Actually, most places Scarlet went
became waggy places.

Happiness can be
kind of contagious.

When Scarlet's parents shared the news
that there'd be a new baby in the family,
it seemed that Scarlet's tail wagged

for nine

months

straight.

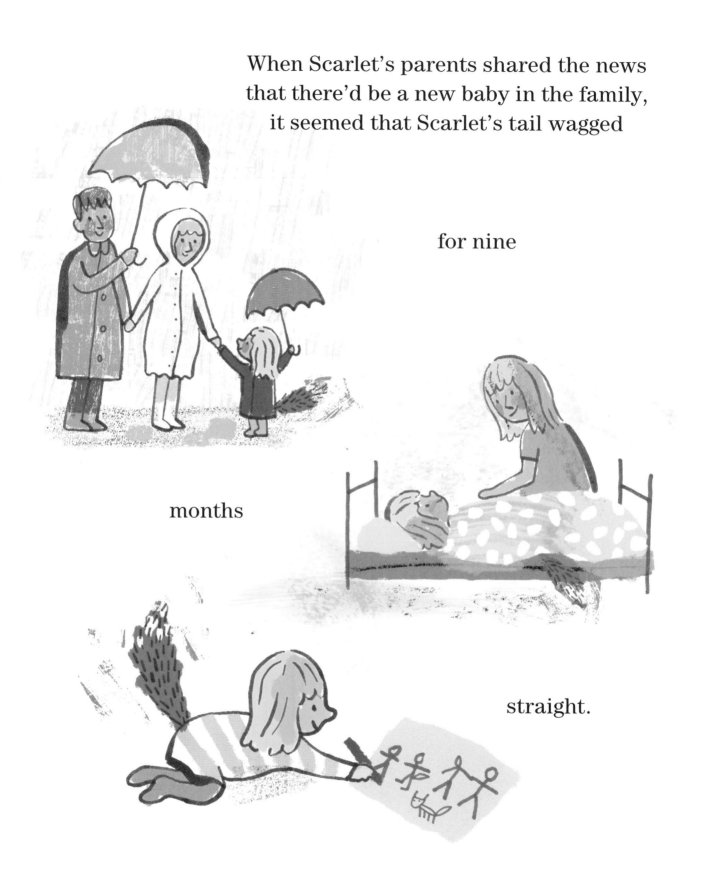

And when her brother was finally born,
it was Scarlet's turn to do
the usual counting:

Ten fingers. Ten toes. Two eyes.
And one long, wiggly, waggly, wonderful . . .

. . . trunk.

That was a surprise.